Halloweena

by
MIRIAM GLASSMAN

illustrated by
VICTORIA ROBERTS

Atheneum Books *for* Young Readers
NEW YORK LONDON TORONTO SYDNEY SINGAPORE

For Emily and Julia, always enchanting
—M. G.

For Joanne and Lara
love, V. R.

Atheneum Books for Young Readers
An imprint of Simon & Schuster Children's Publishing Division
1230 Avenue of the Americas
New York, New York 10020

Book design by Michael Nelson.
The text of this book is set in Alcoholica.
The illustrations are rendered in pen, ink, and watercolor.

Manufactured in China
First Edition
10 9 8 7 6 5 4 3 2 1

LIBRARY OF CONGRESS CATALOGING-IN-PUBLICATION DATA
Glassman, Miriam.
Halloweena / written by Miriam Glassman ; illustrations by Victoria Roberts.
p.   cm.
Summary: Hepzibah the witch raises a baby girl to cast spells and ride a broomstick but the child still wants to be friends with other human children.
ISBN 0-689-82825-X
[1. Witches—Fiction. 2. Halloween—Fiction.] I. Roberts, Victoria, 1957- ill.
PZ7.G4814355 Hal 2002
[E]—dc21   2001041256

Hepzibah
lived in an old tower
and ate nothing but burnt cupcakes.
No one in the neighborhood dared
to speak to her, and children
were warned to stay away
from her door. After
all, she was a
witch.

One day, the mailman brought her a letter.

Dearest Hepzibah,

What a muddle I'm in. You were right about my disappearing vegetables. It was the neighbors, after all! As soon as I discovered them picking my garden clean, I took your advice and demanded their baby in exchange for the Brussels sprouts. Trouble is, I've just met the most enchanting frog, and wouldn't you know, babies give him warts! I tried to return the child, but my pesky neighbors moved away, and neither spell nor crystal ball can find them. You have to help me! You're my only sister, and I'm sure you'll raise her well. Just one request: *Please* keep her away from humans. Those celery-snitching scallywags are nothing but trouble!

The baby will be in your cornfield on Halloween night.

Horrors to you, my dear,

Zillah

"Lizard's gizzards!" Hepzibah sputtered. "I've raised rats, bats, and broccoli, but I've never raised a child!" She was so upset, she left the cauldron bubbling all over her new carpet.

Sure enough, on Halloween night, after her
ride against the moon, Hepzibah stomped
through her old, dry cornfield, and there it was.

"Beetles and bones!" muttered the witch. She poked the baby. The baby smiled.

She scowled at the baby. The baby still smiled.

She glared at the baby with her meanest, beadiest eye. The baby gurgled, and the witch picked her up. "Why, you're as cold as a newt's belly!" she cried, and whisked her inside at once.

"Well, this is a fine kettle of slugs," said Hepzibah. "How's a witch like me supposed to care for an imp like you? I don't suppose you like burnt cupcakes? And what a fright you are. Not a wart on you." The witch sighed. "But you're as cute as a baby bat. And if I can change a fool into a flea, I could certainly change a diaper. But what of Sister's request? Human folk are as thick as weeds around here." She scratched her chin and looked down at the baby. "I wonder, Imp. Any chance you could learn to be a clever little witch?"

The baby burped, and the witch named her Halloweena.

Having a baby around the house meant a lot of changes for Hepzibah. She had to pull all the poison ivy from her garden and plant beans and fruit trees instead. "Well," she sighed, "a tempting apple might be useful now and then."

Finding time to make potions was hard. Sometimes the witch felt as if all she ever conjured up were Lizard Tongue Teething Biscuits. And Halloweena always fussed while Hepzibah stirred the Dragon's Eye Brew. To top it all off, good baby-sitters were hard to find, so Hepzibah gave up her wild nights out with the ghouls. She feared she was going batty.

But somehow, Hepzibah muddled
through and for Halloweena's
third birthday, she gave her
a broom of her very own.
Again and again,
Halloweena tried to fly,
but she always fell down,
scraping her knees, banging
her elbows, or tumbling onto the
cat. Halloweena was miserable.

Hepzibah was at her wits' end. Then one day she saw a boy riding a bicycle, and dashed down to the dungeon.

From then on, Hepzibah and Halloweena rode together on Halloween night. And every year, Halloweena asked about the children below.

"You're not like them," sniffed Hepzibah, mindful of her sister's letter. "They're nothing but trouble."

"But they're small like me," said Halloweena, "and they laugh the same way, too."

"Don't worry," said Hepzibah, "you'll get your cackle soon enough."

Though she still couldn't cackle by the time she was six, Halloweena could burn cupcakes to a crackly crisp and turn the mailman into a kangaroo.

"You're certainly becoming a clever little witch," said Hepzibah. And Halloweena felt proud. But she kept thinking about the children who laughed like her. She was tired of playing with her goblins. The only game they liked was hide-and-shriek.

So the next Halloween night, Halloweena swooped
down on her broom and called out to the children.
It was the only time they ever dared to come near the
tower. But the wind was howling, and they didn't hear her.
Halloweena watched as they crept up to the door, banged
on it, then ran away, laughing. One little girl dropped
some candy.

NO
TREATS
JUST
TRICKS

Halloweena scooped it up and brought it to Hepzibah. "What's this?" she asked.

"Nothing but trouble," said Hepzibah. "Every year those frightful imps try to rattle my bones with their tricks while nosing around for sweets. Throw it away, and come sit with me. I've baked us some fresh lady fingers!"

Halloweena's hand closed around the candy. "No, thank you," she said. "I think I'll just go to bed."

Upstairs, Halloweena pulled the covers over her head.

Then she took a piece of the candy and bit its white tip. "Mmmmm," she hummed. Carefully, Halloweena bit off just the orange part and then the yellow. Piece by piece, she ate the white, the orange, and the yellow till it was all gone. Sitting up, Halloweena scratched her chin, thoughtfully.

Then she
jumped
out of bed
and flew
downstairs.

"Why do we always have to ride against the moon on Halloween?" she demanded. "Why do we always have to sing haunting melodies? Why can't I play with those kids out there? Why can't I be their friend?"

"Because you're a WITCH!" snapped Hepzibah. Halloweena stood stiffly, sniffing back her tears, then ran up to her room.

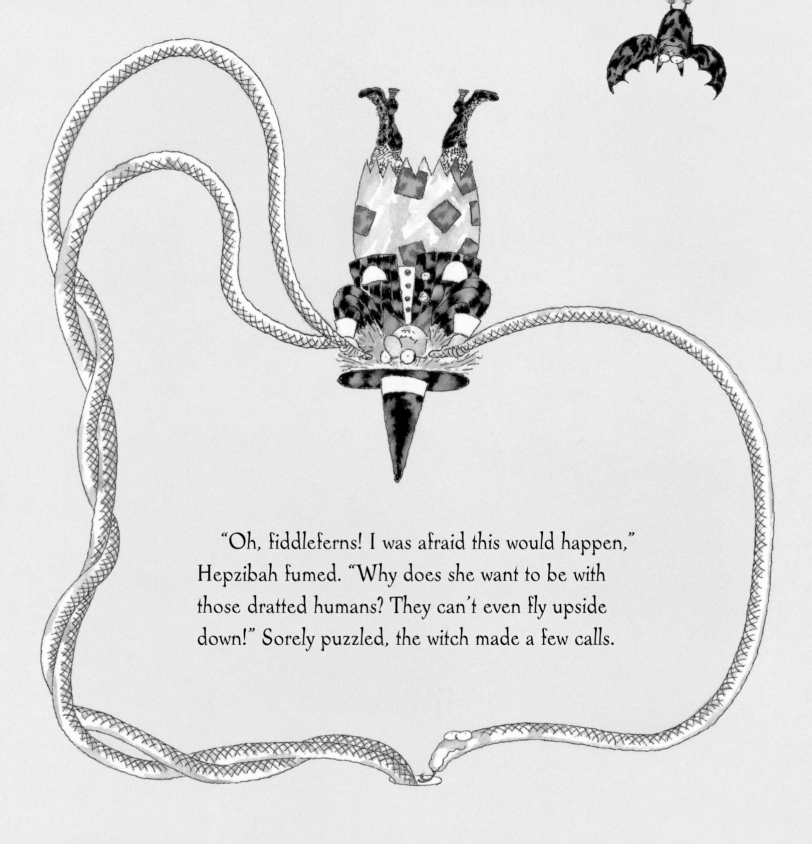

"Oh, fiddleferns! I was afraid this would happen," Hepzibah fumed. "Why does she want to be with those dratted humans? They can't even fly upside down!" Sorely puzzled, the witch made a few calls.

"Lock her in your tower top, and throw away the key," suggested one old crone.

"A spindle prick will put her to sleep for a good, long time," advised another.

"Oh, for goodness sake, just give her to me," urged her friend from the gingerbread house. "I can always use a hand when I have guests for dinner."

But their advice left Hepzibah more vexed than ever.

She couldn't bring herself to lock up little Halloweena. Or have her sleep through every Halloween. And she certainly didn't want to send her away. Yet the more Hepzibah thought about Halloweena feeling lonely, the sadder she became.

"If Halloweena wants playmates, then that's the way it's got to be. Besides, how hard could it be to make a few friends?" So down to the dungeon she flew.

Hepzibah worked her best spells, but all of the friends she made for Halloweena either croaked, slithered, or hopped away. Tired and disenchanted, the witch went up to her room.

But as Hepzibah was climbing into bed, Halloweena was climbing out of hers. She picked up her thickest magic books, and headed outside.

The next morning, Halloweena dashed straight to the cornfield. It was alive again, its gleaming stalks rising high into the sky. Hundreds of white-tipped candies peeked out from the leaves, and children were rushing into the field to get them. Halloweena ran to welcome them, and a little girl smiled at her.

"Look!" said the little girl. "We have the same missing tooth!"

"I got three frogs for my tooth," replied Halloweena. "How many did you get?"

A boy with a mouthful of candy ran up to Halloweena. "This is better than trick-or-treat!" he said. "Can you grow a bubble-gum bush, too?"

Suddenly, the children froze. There, at the edge of the
field, stood Hepzibah.

"Slithering snakes! What's all this?" The witch hobbled
closer. She poked a stalk. She scowled. She stared with her
beadiest eye. "A candy-corn field?!" cried Hepzibah, and she
cackled loud and long. Then she turned to Halloweena.
"You're a mighty clever witch to conjure this up. But what
are we going to do with all these candy-snitching scamps?"

"I think we should have a Halloween party," said
Halloweena.

"But Halloween was yesterday," said the girl with the
missing tooth.

Hepzibah scratched her chin thoughtfully. "Then this,"
she declared, "will be a Halloweena party!"

And so it was.